LET'S BE CONFIDANTE

I THINK, I SHOULD BURN YOUR LOVE IN FIRE OF MY HEART.

AARCHI ADVANI SAINI

ISBN 979-888521863-4

Contents

"let's Be Confidante"

By Aarchi Advani Saini.!

Author

Aarchi Advani Saini.!

[ ] Author of the book "The Loads Of Poetry"

[ ] Social media "Aarchi Advani"

[ ] Aries, believe in destiny.

Aarchi was born in India on 25th March 2002, the daughter of Sanjeev Advani Saini(an engineer) and his wife Mamta Saini (a homemaker).

She becomes one of the youngest author of Shamli. So renowned for "The loads of poetry). She has sold the book worldwide, the recipient of numerous prestigious awards in her writing journey. She writes daily columns syndicated throughout the world. Aarchi Advani is well known for her writing on many other platforms. And overthrowing mankind. She is also a fantasy and literary fiction author specializing in "Life".

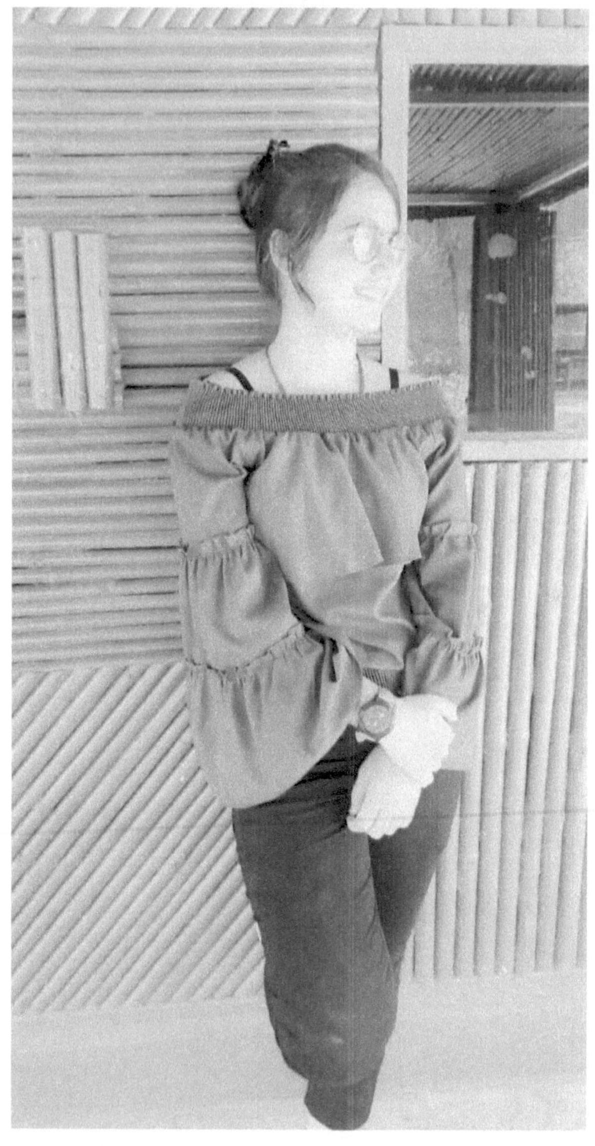

The Aarchi Advani Saini, also hosts a channel where she uses her passion for storytelling. And a background in business to help other creatives navigate their writing. And publishing journey. When she's not writing or tubing she enjoys listening to books,
Making stories on her own. And love to live in her virtual world

1

"Vasanth!", The owner and the chef of Joey's restaurant called him as walked out of the building. The restaurant and the building were side by side. And as it happened, the owner whom Vasanth called Tia was also the landlady of a small rooftop flat that Vasanth rented. Tia and Vasanth had with time, become a family away from family and as such it was their morning custom to share a cup of tea before the day drew on and work piled on.

Today was no exception. Vasanth took a seat opposite Tia who was already seated on the restaurant tables on the pavement.

"Good morning Tia", he said pleasantly.

Tia smiled and asked one of her staff to bring tea for both of them.

In the few minutes that they sat waiting for their tea, they talked about the general topics that occupied their minds, of the weather and the upcoming festivities. Once the tea arrived both resigned to enjoy its warmth in content silence.

Towards the end of the tea, the postman arrived, earlier than expected. Seeing Tia outside, the postman handed her three envelopes and then rummaged his bag until he found another one.

Tia looked over her letters as the postman took his leave.

She went through each of the first three letters carefully. Two of them were the electricity and gas bills whereas the last one was an invitation to judge a culinary competition in the locality. During this time, Vasanth scrolled through his notifications, uninterested in any.

Tia reached for the fourth envelope and then stopped.

"It's for you", she said, noticing the name on the envelope.

"What? Me?", Vasanth sounded astonished. "Is it from the University?"

Tia glanced at the sender's address. And shook her head.

"Let me see", he took the letter from her hand.

"There's an address but no name."

"Open it", Tia urged.

Carefully, Vasanth tore open the envelope and the letter fell out onto the table. Tia shifted her chair close to his as Vasanth unfolded and paper. Together they began to read.

'It's the beginning of the monsoon. I can already feel it in the air around me. The cold that soothes, that despite its nature, warms.

I see the clouds gather around the mountains through my window, as time moves by they completely cloak it such that I can no longer see the mountains but only a pure white, where the mountains were supposed to be.

The thunder has begun, slowly the first drop of rain will meet the earth and others will follow. Suddenly you can no longer hear your surroundings except the rain and the thunder. It soothes me. Doesn't it soothe you too??

The dark melancholy that sometimes follows the rain calms me. No, I am not deranged. But rain and thunder make me feel small, all the worldly problems suddenly feel trivial.

The lightning strikes

And suddenly, there's strength to handle life. To face the world.

Flowers have started to bloom, the grass has begun to conquer the barren land. The rain had done its job and now, the sun peaks out. And just like that the mystic magic of rain now feels like a dream.

A dream of rain and thunder.

I am going with the flow of thoughts here but have you ever felt like breaking into a dance the moment you vibe with a song. A free-flowing rhythm that grips your soul, insulated from the world through the mortal shells of flesh, unable to break free, unable to dance to the rhythm.

I feel that every time I vibe with a song. But I am not a dancer, I can't twirl with the rhythm so instead, I feel it. I feel it and I dream, allowing the soul to explore itself, unhindered, to roam.

Perhaps, I am too vague, too distant for you to understand me.

So I'll stop here, until the time is right, until next time, until you ask me to write back.

Truly,

A someone.

P.S. Yes, we are strangers never formally introduced but I have heard about you. I know you, well at least the address; enough to send a letter with a peek into my mind. Whether to reply or not is a choice that you have. But know that, I'm just someone wanting to have a connection with someone without the shackles of outings, WhatsApp and media.

Both Vasanth and Tia read the letter, unsure where it was going. The letter ended with an equally subtle salutation and wanting more, Vasanth turned the page over to find the postscript.

He read it aloud so Tia could hear it, who had once more shifted her chair, only this time away from him.

"What do you think?", he asked.

" What do I think? Uff… it's something. Who writes letters these days..", Tia replied, now returning her letters into the envelope they came in.

"That's it? But her descriptions…they are so apt, so different. Her state of mind is so different… it's like it's here concerning itself with petty things and in the next moments, it's worrying about the universe. Like a….dreamer does."

Tia smiled, "You think it's her?"

"I guess", he shrugged.

" You seem interested. Going to reply, I suppose."

Vasanth paused for a second before answering, "I don't know. Will it be an idea if I do?"

Tia said nothing but instead asked for the envelope to see the address. Vasanth handed it to her. She read the address and then squinted her eyes as she thought something. Then taking her phone she typed something on it.

"Ah…here we go.", she said as she handed the phone to Vasanth to see.

Vasanth needed only to glance at the screen to know that it was currently displaying the map of the locality, with a pin pointing at a particular place.

" What's this?", he asked.

"That's the address from where the letter came. It's a cookery shop owned by Mrs Murti, a nice old lady; I have known her for many years now. You could go there and ask about the letter if you are confused. Maybe find the person, see if you are interested. And if yes, get their number…"

Vasanth scoffs. "Faster than letters", she says mischievously.

Saying so, she headed inside and Vasanth shoved the letter in his bag. He, too, left.

As the subway station drew nearer the letter slipped from his mind, instead all his attention was focused on the shop. Vasanth worked in Pinto's repair. A shop that not only sold electronics but also had hand in their repairs. Vasanth worked part time here, but since University wouldn't be starting for another two weeks, he had started to work full time. His education stream in the university allowed him a slight advantage when it came to the repairs. Pinto, the owner and Vansaths employer had a policy that he could take anything from the trash if he thought he could make it work. Thus Vasanth got the equipment he used for his experiments in a very cheaper way.

Today, as his boss was away, Vasanth was tasked with the sole responsibility of managing the shop with another one of the employees who worked full time there, Raghu.

The morning at the shop proved to be a busy one, both had to go through the inventory, manage the trash disposal, sweep the shop and repair the few equipment and household machines that had come during the previous day.

Thus the morning and afternoon passed with work and customers. It was not until evening that they had nothing to do. Raghu being not much of a talker, the conversation always ended abruptly by Raghu nodding a reply or monosyllabic answers.

Thus then his mind found its way back to that morning, to the letter. Something about it intrigued him. It inspired a curiosity, a deep want to know more of that person's mind. Of that person themselves. Much to his annoyance he found himself wondering, what sort of person they are? The spiritual kind or the dreamer poet kind? Are they old or?

He forcefully stopped the questions. Afterall, they are nonsense, he declared. And yet not find minutes later, he found himself typing the address in the search bar of the map.

As the day drew to an end, Vasanth was glad to leave the shop and returned to his small flat cut into the roof. He liked it there. It was big and comfortable enough for him. And the rent was cheap.

Once home the task of cooking himself dinner threw all thoughts to the wind and Vasanth had quite dinner binge watching a comedy movie.

But humans by nature are curious people. Once a doubt, a thing enters their mind that inspires curiosity, it gets impossible to remove it. You have to do something to satisfy this urge and Vasanth was no exception to this.

Late at night, he found himself at his study table, the letter to infront and he wondered if he should reply. Then in a sudden impulse pulled out a blank sheet and a pen from the drawer and stared at it, under the light of the table lamp, unsure.

But dark clouds don't necessarily guarantee showers. Staring at a blank sheet does not guarantee words to imprint on it. Will Vasanth succumb to the curiosity about the person and write a letter to a complete stranger?

2

A few days before Vasanth received his letter:

"What are you writing?", Dadi-maa asked as she sat reading in the courtyard between her shop and her house. She lived there with her granddaughters.

"Letter... I mean Nothing", answered her eldest granddaughter.

Dadi-ma scrutinized the eldest.

" Shouldn't you be...what is it called again..ah! Texting your friends?", she asked.

The eldest daughter, a twenty-something girl, who looked much older and mature for her age answered, "They are not friends at least I won't call them that. Just some people I went to school with. And I feel like an outsider amongst them especially when they start talking about some singer I have never heard of or movies I am not interested in. The conclusion: not my type. Too pretentious. Can't even see their thoughts."

Saying so she got back to scribbling on the piece of paper.

"What are you going to do then?"

"Find a correspondence of course. Someone willing to listen"

Saying so she left the room. Watching her leave, Dadi-maa thought, 'Like mother like daughter.'

The day after Vasanth receives the letter.

Vasanth and Tia are having their tea, sitting outside, as was their custom. But today, Tia's twelve-year-old daughter, Mindy, had joined them. While the other two sipped their tea, Mindy stared at the glass of milk, as she munched her cookies.

"What's that?", she asked Vasanth, pointing at the white envelope in the pocket of his jacket, lying on the table, opposite her.

"Nothing", he replies, picking up the jacket and placing it on his lap. Averting his eyes from Tia's who's sharp gaze had seen the envelope.

" You wrote back didn't you?", she asked, having no intention to mask the note of surprise from her voice.

"Yes", Vasanth replied, still looking down.

"What did you write?", asked the curious kid.

"He received a letter yesterday. Today he's replying.", Tia answered while Vasanth looked up, his face reddening.

" Love letter ?!", Jumped the kid.

"What! No!"

Then, the adults burst into laughter, much to the annoyance of the kid who thought a big secret was kept from her, and sat down once more with a sulking face.

"I was curious", Vasanth said, feeling the need to explain himself, " Seemed like that person had a lot to tell..."

"And you felt like you could listen to..well whoever they are?", asked Tia.

Vasanth nodded in reply.

" I can understand. To think of it, yes, it did seem like they had a lot to talk about."

"Who had?", asked the kid.

"We..don't know", answered Vasanth.

Mindy looked puzzled. Expecting an explanation. But none came.

" Now, go post it", Tia said with a smile as she began picking up their empty cups.

"Yes", he stood up, put his jacket back on and left, Mindy, calling behind him, " GET ME A CHOCOLATE"

"WILL DO".

Two days later, Mrs Murti's shop received a letter, addressed from Joey's.

A twenty-something girl got hold of it before anyone could see it on the shop counter. Carefully, taking it into the light, she tore open the envelope. And the letter fell onto the table. She began unfolding it but- she heard someone calling her. Quickly hiding the letter among the many other things on her table. She ran down the stairs.

Later that night, in the light of her table lamp, she began to read the letter. It said-

'Greetings,

I don't know who you are. Neither where you are. Nor do I know your name or what you look like. And I am fine with not knowing these things.

Because you see I am starting to see you, even know you perhaps, through your words. Now, you might think that words are just words, void perhaps. But they are not. You see, the way we use these seemingly innocent words betrays a lot about who one is.

I never liked the rain. Everything is damp and soaked. Buses are late, potholes suddenly emerge and no matter how careful you walk under the raincoat or the umbrella, you have to get a little drenched by the rain before you reach wherever you want to. That's its rule. And there are seldom exceptions. I don't like that.

But now, your words and essentially your thoughts have shown me a different side of the rain. It's like I have started seeing the notorious kid for who he really is: a kid.

Somewhat of a rationalized view, I have. But I am curious too. So who are you?

Something tells me I might not get an answer. So I won't ask again. I'd listen to the voice your words have. They too might betray your identity someday.

But I don't want you to write back just because I am curious. No. But because I have a feeling; you want to talk but more importantly to be heard; to let your thoughts out into the world, something I guess you seldom do.

So the only question you can answer is, will you write back?

Truly,

A stranger.'

A faint smile climbed onto her lips as she folded the letter back, returning it to its envelope. For a few minutes, she sat there still, staring through her window; looking at nothing particular, seeing the light of the streetlamp seep into the room. Then jolting she picked up her writing pad and began scribbling.

Two days later, Vasanth received another letter one morning. He began to read-

'The arrival announced the answer.

Can you paint? I can't. Yet every time there's a scenery around me I can't help but want to paint. Or to be converted in an instant into some old oil painting or a Polaroid blurred by the passage of time.

The reason why I am saying all this and will probably say more is simple. There's this room, whose gloomy ambience is comforting. The singular window it has is permanently covered with a sheet, such that one cannot see what's beyond. And yet, the sun rays creep in. Slowly and decisively. Unhampered. It creates a nice contrast in this otherwise dark room. The light penetrates the darkness, slowly dispersing itself so that the room is no longer dark. The gloom retreated itself into the corners. Can you picture it?

It has a certain vibe, a timelessness if you will, that spellbinds you once you step inside.

It reminds me of a period, where one would sit in such a room, overlooking through a window, a vast expanse of land covered with carefully planted shrubberies and the wilderness that's just beyond the compound, inborn in nature; perhaps then, the window isn't covered. A faint song is being carried through the wind and you sit there lost in your own bubble, reading under the faint scent of a scented candle or perhaps writing a letter.

An ideal, laid back condition for a dreamer to dream on. Isn't it? I am such a dreamer. What do I dream of? What does anyone dream of really? Everything one has always wished for. Maybe that's why we like creating fake scenarios that are always in our favour. Gives us power, control that we think we lack in our lives. But it's a false sense. A hoax.

There is order and chaos but no ultimate control over either. The light might sneak inside, things might brighten, but the darkness that looms in the corner fights for the chaos.

Each has an upper hand sometimes. But not ultimate control. It's always changing like the phases of the moon. We are like the window, that must always learn to carry both light and darkness. Order and chaos.

After all, we each have our demons to battle. And so do I, something called self-doubt and fear.

Truly,

Someone,

Willing to acknowledge her downfalls and to listen in turn.'

Thus, one letter leads to another and then another. Until it becomes a part of their lives, sharing each time a little part of their being; observing as the burdens they carried along slowly became lighter.

The fear and self-doubt were slowly steadily, battled with belief, the rain began to be less whined about.

But everything comes to an end, a few flowers don't necessarily mean the tree isn't drying. A few changes don't necessarily bring you to the other side. There's a long way to go. So just as Vasanth thought, he understood 'someone', a letter makes him doubt himself.

'It's mid-July', it read, 'One cannot escape the dark gloomy clouds for long now. It is catching up with me. I feel it all; isolation, loneliness, and solitude all at once. Like three different personalities are trying to get control. Each, trying to get control. I'm surrounded by people I care about and yet at times, I can't reach them. It's like I'm back in the room, overlooking the expanse of land, only my voice is too far away to be heard, words too foreign to be understood..'

3

'It drives me crazy...', The letter continued.

'..at times, this feeling of not being understood, of being unable to reach. The walls then begin to feel claustrophobic a moment; the next, they seem to go on forever, drawing out the sense of being the only living soul. Then, the room seems to return to its original dimensions. I hear merry voices, laughing and giggling. And I try to open the door, to join them, but the door doesn't budge. I panic. And then, I blink, returning back to my own room, the window of which overlooks not the land, but the street. Those feelings ebb but never die.

I'm still fearful and self-doubting I have won but small victories. The important ones are but a mammoth of a battle.

I need to get rid of them once and for all, at whatever cost. After all, growth doesn't mean anything if the seeds of fear are buried deep within. And hence, I need to eradicate the self-destructive poison of self-doubt and fear. Only then will the shackles break and the demons be banished.

Call it an exorcism, a rebirth or a beginning of an incredible journey, regardless, it needs to be done, sooner.

It's not much of a living when I am frustrated most times and on the paths of self-harm the other times.

See you then, on the other side.

Truly,

Someone, finally courageous enough.'

Vasanth couldn't understand, he simply couldn't fathom the meaning. Had it been from someone else he would have ruled it out as absurd. But not now. By now, he had learned to look between the lines, to understand more than the words conveyed. And yet, he couldn't; not with this one. The words felt ominous, even desperate on the paper as he read them over and over again until he knew them by heart.

He penned down a response, in all the words he could employ to draw out a brighter, more hopeful life for the reader; His sneaky way, as means of saying 'no' to whatever destructive thoughts gripped the sender. By afternoon, the response was posted.

This brought in a small fraction of relief for him, but not all, he was still concerned, afraid the damage was already done before his letter could reach.

One morning, after several days, Tia asked, "You have been looking uneasy all week Vasanth, is everything alright?"

Vasanth looked up at her, his fingers moving along the rim of the cup. He could see in her eyes the concern she had over his behaviour lately. A pang of guilt sprung up from somewhere within

"Sorry..it's nothing", he replied.

And yet, he could feel her gaze upon him. He took a deep breath and decided to tell her the truth. He removed the letter from his pocket and passed it to her. He carried it along with him. In what hopes or for what reasons, we might never know

Tia took it from him, eyeing it suspiciously, before unfolding the paper and beginning to read it.

"Exorcism? Rebirth? What's going on?" She asked minutes later, confusion clear on her face.

"Those are just metaphors…. think…I hope", Vasanth replied. Tia looked at him, waiting for him to explain.

He sighed as he replied, "Usually, there are a lot of metaphors and comparisons. But that's not the point..", he stopped, then he asked, "Doesn't it seem ominous to you?"

Tia glanced at the letter and then nodded. "Ominous might be a strong word. But it's left me unsettled, that's for sure. Did you get a reply?"

"No. I replied the very same day. I should have had the reply at least by Friday. But it will be one week tomorrow since last Friday and I can't help but feel worried. I know it's illogical but I can't help it. I walked by the address twice in the last two days. But I couldn't make myself walk inside the shop. I was…"

"Afraid?", Tia said softly, pitying Vasanth.

He nodded.

"In that case, would you be afraid even if I accompanied you?"

"No. You'll do that?", He asked eagerly.

"Yes", Tia smiled. "Let's go."

Mrs Murti's shop had just opened. Her youngest granddaughter, Ruhi, a teenager, was reading the morning newspaper behind the counter when the jingling of the bells caused by the opening of the door made her abandon her paper, walk out front.

"Welcome! How can I help you?", she asked cheerfully.

Vasanth, surprised to see Ruhi, looked around himself, words failing him in his endeavour to explain the cause behind his agitation and visit. He had asked Tia to wait outside out of some conceptions of the embarrassment. But now he wished she was here, answering the questions of this girl, who had now proceeded to ask what crockery he needed.

"I...um...I was looking for..", he stammered suddenly realising that he had no name for the person about whose wellbeing he was worried about. He was aware of the girl's eyes on him, curious they were. He removed the letter from his pocket and in an equally quick moment replaced it back.

"Never mind. It was a mistake". His face reddened as he turned towards the door.

No sooner had he walked further than two steps, that something dawned on Ruhi.

"Wait!" She called.

Vasanth turned around, eyes questioning.

"Just wait. Please. I'll be back" she said earnestly as she rushed off through the door behind the counter, calling "Dadi-maa!", into what could be only assumed to be Mrs Murti's residence.

"What's going on?", Tia asked, having arrived by Vasanth's side after hearing Ruhi calling for Dadi-maa at the top of her voice.

Vasanth filled her in with what had happened so far, which wasn't much so they passed the time by looking at the shelves, waiting for Ruhi to return.

Mrs Murti or as she was to her granddaughters, Dadi-maa, smiled at Tia as she walked in. Tia had been one of her frequent customers and the two shared a friendly relation. Then, she scrutinized Vasanth from head to toe, before smiling at him.

It was her, who spoke first.

"I was starting to wonder if you'd show up. But at last, here you are."

She said, taking his hand in hers. "I am happy to see you, Vasanth", she said, affectionately patting his hand, before moving away.

"Thank you ...I..", Vasanth stammered. While Tia looked from Vasanth to Mrs Murti and back again at him.

"Ruhi", Mrs Murti said with a nod.

Ruhi extended her hand towards Vasanth, a black leather-bound journal in her hand.

"Take it", Mrs Murti encouraged. "It belongs to my oldest daughter. She left it for you. I'm sure you know her."

Still puzzled, Vasanth opened the journal to its first page.

A familiar handwriting greeted him. A name was scrawled on the page, in a firm hand that ironically wrote in a messy font; the letters, sometimes tilting to the left and then at times, to the right.

'Shangun', it read.

"Shagun", Vasanth murmured, the words felt strange and foreign to him; a difficult task to associate this new name to the hand that had crafted the messy font.

"I believe she wrote to you".

Vasanth nodded. No one spoke until Vasanth managed to look up and ask, "But where is ...Shagun? Has something bad..", he couldn't fathom what might have happened.

"She's alright", assured Mrs Murti. "Turn to the next page".

Vasanth did as told. The words written were to the effect as follows-

"For so long, I have hidden in the background. Never wanting to be the centre of anything. Locked myself up amongst the pages of some book as I daydreamed about the world; always doubting myself.

But now, I have finally confessed my downfalls and started to accept them. There is no lock now. But the door is still shut tight. And I am leaving in a self-imposed isolation that at times feels of solitude and at times of loneliness.

I feel a jumble of emotions and thoughts in me; of hatred and compassion; of optimism and pessimism; all growing and spreading, morphing and withering away. Am I then a wild expanse of land where weeds grow just as strong as the tree or am I that expanse where the tree is struggling to be superior to the weeds? I don't know.

And so I have decided to go on a self-prescribed journey; an attempt to discover myself as well as the world I so firmly avoided and yet continued to Desire.

I am going where the road will lead, where the heart might seek and where I won't stay as long as the time required to receive a letter.

So, trusting my feeling about you and knowing that you might come home looking for me. I am leaving you my journal, hoping it answers your questions until I return.

So long then, stranger

Truly…"

The word 'Someone' at the subscription of the letter was struck through; instead, this time it was signed off as Shagun.

After a minute or so Vasanth asked, "She's really gone then?" He closed the journal and gripped it such that his knuckles turned white

Mrs Murti nodded, a sad smile had begun to tug the corners of her wrinkled face.

"Are you going to read it?"Tia asked after they had left the shop to return back to Joey's.

Vasanth, who was continuing to walk by her side, simply looked up towards the sky, instead of answering her.

4

As Vasanth walked home with the journal in his hand, his spirits were just as clouded as the sky above him. The lightning struck, threatening the onset of heavy showers. But When it finally did pour, the night had fallen; the heavens burst open and the rain tormented.

Inside his room, Vasanth could hear the downpour; the deafening patter of it against the rooftops and window panes. He stood by the window, listening, eyes following the movement of water drops onto the window.

A thought sprung in his mind, and he smiled thinking of the mountains that now could be almost hidden, not just by the darkness of the night, but by the dark clouds that brought this downpour.

Eyeing the black journal, Vasanth opened it. Once more, the familiar curves of handwriting met his eyes. He flicked a page randomly. Curiously enough, the entries were not separated by dates, as one would naturally expect, they were separated, in fact by a band of asterisk, which in themselves were oddly shaped; as if the hand that wrote them, couldn't produce one asterisk similar to another.

Vasanth read the entry, that appeared on that page-

'It's one of these sleepless nights, where my thoughts have sabotaged every attempt of drifting asleep. I hear them loud and clear. Troubling, it is, to have your subconscious play this mean game with you; a game where not you, but your thoughts are the Master.'

He read another entry-

'I ran into a group of classmates today at the cafe. Ironically, after all these years when invited to join them, I still managed to fade into the background, Just as I did during school and the subsequent college days.

I had forgotten how I felt back then. How the comparison that had somehow been imbibed into me made me feel inferior; lacking in several aspects when compared to all my very efficient classmates. I feared being the outsider, someone at whose expense laughs were earned. I realize now that even when school had ended long ago, I still held onto that feeling; A constant fear of being mocked, once my back was turned.

Maybe that's why I am afraid of having company. Afraid that within their hearts of hearts they too will make fun of me.'

'Every day feels the same,' began another entry a few pages later. 'Days have started to merge into one another with very few nuances between them. I keep longing for a change of scenario. Twice this week, I have stepped onto a bus leaving the town. Twice I have stepped down even before the bus left the station. I don't dare to face the change. And yet I keep desiring it.'

'Wrath. Another of the seven deadly sins; the one that has enslaved me since long gone, showing itself when the situation made it least necessary. I can't help but wonder, what am I truly angry at? The situation or my inability to change it? I decide on the latter. After all, I feel helpless.

Wild fury fills me during these moments. My hands itch to destroy something but instead, they pick up a blade. The metal feels cold against my skin. A shiver runs through me.

A split second later there is a long scar, the size of my finger; red and stingy, red spots surrounding it. But it doesn't bleed. I fail; even when it comes to harm. '

Vasanth stared at the words, breathless. Words have power, he always believed that. But do words have this much effect too? For even in the roaring thunder outside, he felt he heard the words as if they were spoken to him, laced in every emotion that occupied the speaker's mind.

He continued to read further.

"The sun's just peeking out from over the horizon. The sky has hues of orange, yellow and red scattered across. A cold breeze blows inside just as I open the window. There's a silence hanging in the air, the silence that precedes the waking of the world. It's beautiful. And I can only click a picture; the very first picture taken from the Polaroid I bought yesterday. I am pinning it to this very page, once I finish what I have to say.

In the last few days, I have realised a few things. One of them is that I can feel loneliness, isolation and solitude; all three things. My existence shouldn't be defined by any one of them. I am allowed to experience them. They are important to cherish companionship.

But if I don't allow them to define me then what defines me? Fear, I have realised, is too commonplace to be associated with individual identity; looks, beauty, too short-lived; mind, always fluctuating. What then defines us? Defines me?

I am starting to believe that in the end, it's only two things that matter; two things that can do some justice towards defining the complexity of a person. Coward or brave.

Is a person brave enough to walk against all odds, to risk everything just so they could find the joy in their life or are they coward enough to suffer at the hands of life?

My cowardice has been a part of me for too long, making me afraid of stepping out of my comfort zone. But amazing things happen beyond this zone, don't they?

And so I am stepping out. Both of this metaphysical zone and this town; a self-prescribed journey. Finally, leaving, to explore the world, like Mom once did, like I always wanted to.

Goodbye,

For now. '

Vasanth unpinned the Polaroid of the morning sky that was pinned there and smiled as he saw the hues of the sky.

'You stepped out of your zone a long time ago, even before you realised it..', he thought, '..by sending the letter'.

The next day, he returned the journal to Mrs Murti, but not before scribbling something at the bottom of the Polaroid.

'When you do return, I hope you found what you so desired.'

What happens next? Does she come back? Do they meet? Does she write once more? Is it the end of their correspondence? One can only imagine the answers. Perhaps then, there might be a story for another time. Perhaps not.

Maybe it's one of those stories that do not desire a conclusive end; That is always happening. Always progressing. At times apart, and at times together. But never-ending. After all, how can we meet them again if it's the end?

So let's not call it a goodbye but instead, Adiós for now.